for Laura

First published in Great Britain in 2001 by Andersen Press Ltd., 20 Vauxhall Bridge Road,
London SW1V 2SA. Published in Australia by Random House Australia Pty.,
20 Alfred Street, Milsons Point, Sydney, NSW 2061. All rights reserved.
Colour separated in Switzerland by Photolitho AG, Zürich.
Printed and bound in Italy by Grafiche AZ, Verona.

10   9   8   7   6   5   4   3   2   1

British Library Cataloguing in Publication Data available.

ISBN   1 84270 032 4

This book has been printed on acid-free paper

Horrible Hair

Written and illustrated
by Gerald Rose

Andersen Press
London

Lion had been invited to a riverboat party but he wasn't happy.

"What horrible hair I have!" he moaned.
"I must do something about it."

He brushed it, he combed it, he curled it.
He tried it this way and that . . .

. . . but he still didn't like his horrible hair.
"I'll ask my friends what *they* think . . ." said Lion.

"Hippo, what do you think of my horrible hair?"
"I can't look at your hair now. I'm getting ready
for the party," said Hippo.

"Elephant, do you like my horrible hair?"
"Don't make me laugh," said Elephant. "I'm trying
to paint my toe-nails."

"Mandrill, what can I do with my horrible hair?"
"Wash it and comb it and get rid of those curls.
They look like noodles," sniggered Mandrill.

"Snake, do you like the colour of my horrible hair?"
"I liked it much better when it was pink," said Snake.

"Warthog, do you think I should go to the party with my horrible hair like this?"
"Go away!" squealed Warthog. "You gave me such a fright I've smudged my lipstick."

"Oh, dear!" sniffed Lion. "I really do have horrible hair, and they are all laughing at me."
Leopard banged on his drum. "Come on, Lion. Forget about your hair. Get on the riverboat. The party has started."

The riverboat chugged up the river.

"I hope my hair doesn't get wet," sighed Lion.

The band played. The music got louder and louder.
Everybody danced . . . except Lion.

"Come and join us," croaked Crocodile.
"I can't," wailed Lion. "I might spoil my hair."

"Look at me! I'm a good dancer," boasted Elephant.
"So am I," called Hippo.

He jumped higher and higher. He wouldn't stop.

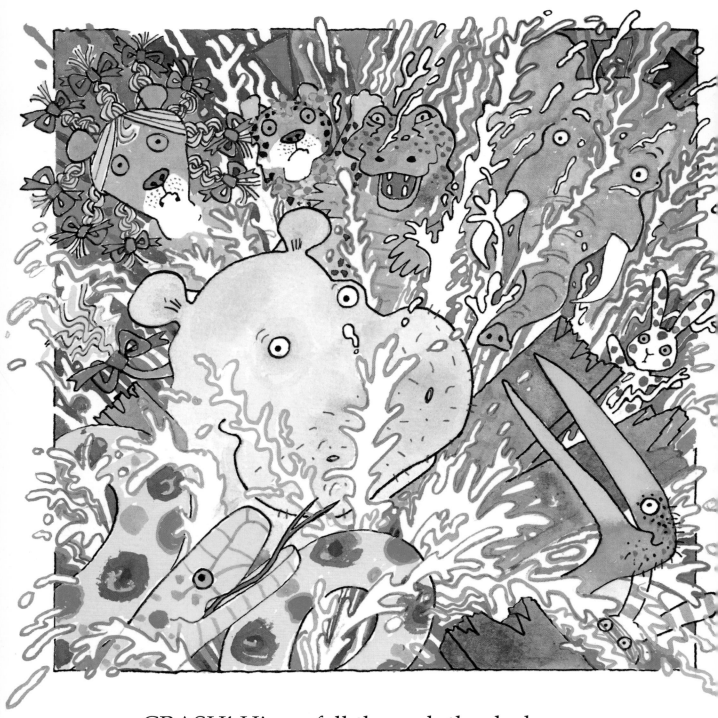

CRASH! Hippo fell through the deck.
WHOOSH! There was water everywhere.

As the riverboat sank, Lion dived into the water.

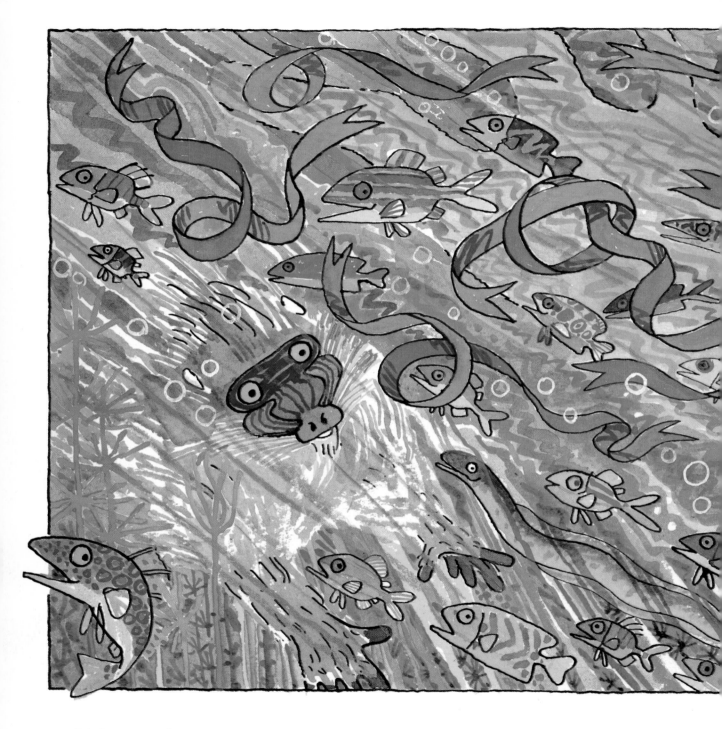

"What a disaster!" he thought. "I'm losing my ribbons . . .

. . . and my hair will be even more HORRIBLE!"

Miserably, Lion climbed up the muddy bank . . .
"Look at Lion's hair!" yelled Hippo.
"Don't make fun of me," wept Lion. "I know I look a mess."

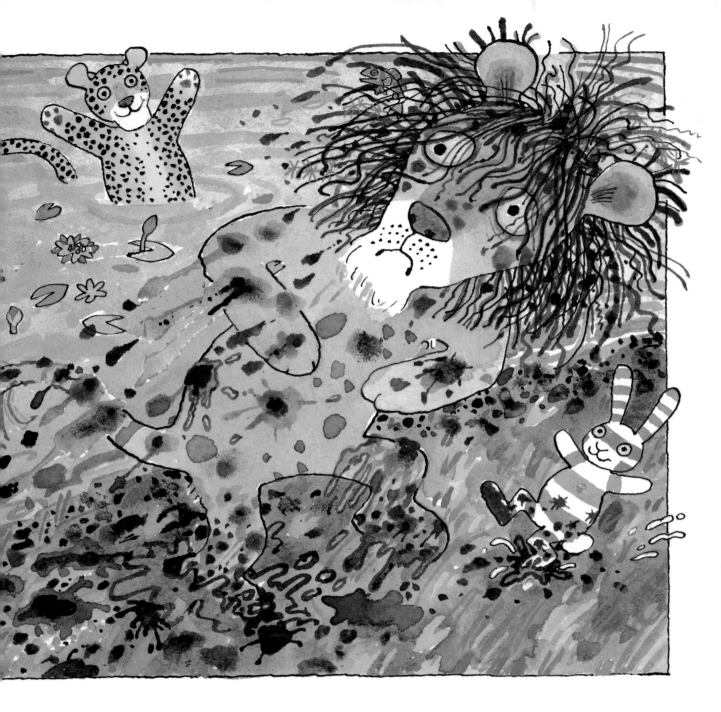

"No you don't," cried all his friends. "You look WONDERFUL!"
"Do I?" gasped Lion.
"Yes!" they shouted. "That's the best hairstyle you have had all day."

"Oh, thank you!" sighed Lion,
and he smiled for the very first time.
"I'll never worry about my horrible hair again.
Now let's get on with the party!" he roared.

And that is *exactly* what they did . . .